Frog is frightened

Frog is frightened

Max Velthuijs

Andersen Press · London

Frog was very frightened. He was lying in bed, and he could hear strange noises everywhere. There was a creaking in the cupboard and a rustling under the floorboards.
"Somebody is under my bed," thought Frog.

He jumped out of bed and ran through the dark woods until he reached Duck's house.

"How nice of you to come and see me," said Duck. "But it is rather late. I'm about to go to bed."

"Please, Duck," said Frog. "I'm frightened. There's a ghost under my bed."

"Nonsense," laughed Duck. "There's no such thing."
"There is," said Frog. "The woods are haunted as well."
"Don't be frightened," said Duck. "You can stay with me. I'm not afraid."
And they huddled into bed together. Frog cuddled Duck's warm body and wasn't frightened any more.

All of a sudden they heard a scratching noise on the roof.
"What was that?" asked Duck, sitting up with a jolt.
The next moment they heard a creaking on the stairs.
"This house is haunted too!" shouted Frog. "Let's get out
of here."
And they ran out into the woods.

Frog and Duck ran as fast as they could.

They felt there were ghosts and scary monsters everywhere.

Eventually they reached Pig's house and, gasping for breath, they hammered on the door.

"Who is it?" asked a sleepy voice.

"Please, Pig, open the door. It's us," shouted Frog and Duck.

"What's the matter?" asked Pig angrily. "Why have you woken me up in the middle of the night?"

"Please help us," said Duck. "We're terrified. The woods are full of ghosts and monsters."

Pig laughed. "What nonsense. Ghosts and monsters don't exist. You know that."

"Well, look for yourself," said Frog.

Pig looked out of the window, but he couldn't see anything
unusual.
"Please, Pig, may we sleep here? We're so scared."
"O.K.," said Pig. "My bed is big enough. And I am never
frightened. I don't believe in all that rubbish."

So there they were, all three of them together in Pig's bed.
"This is nice," thought Frog. "Nothing can happen now."
But they couldn't sleep. They listened to all the strange,
frightening noises in the woods. This time, Pig heard them too!

But luckily the three friends could comfort each other. They shouted out that they were not scared - that they weren't afraid of anything. Eventually they fell asleep exhausted.

Next morning, Hare went to visit Frog. The door was wide
open and Frog was nowhere to be seen.
"This is strange," thought Hare.

Duck's house was also empty.

"Duck, Duck, where are you?" shouted Hare. But there was no answer. Hare was very worried. He thought something terrible must have happened.

Terrified, he ran through the woods looking for Frog and Duck.
He looked and looked but there was no trace of his friends.
"Perhaps Pig will know where they are," he thought.

Hare knocked on Pig's door. There was no answer. It was very quiet. He looked in through the window and there he saw his three friends lying in bed, fast asleep. It was ten o'clock in the morning! Hare knocked on the window.

"Help! A ghost!" shouted the three friends.
Then they saw that it was Hare.

Pig unlocked the door and they all ran outside.
"Oh, Hare," they said. "We were so frightened. The wood is full of ghosts and scary monsters."
"Ghosts and monsters?" said Hare surprised. "They don't exist."

"How do you know?" said Frog angrily. "There was one under my bed."

"Did you see it?" asked Hare quietly.

"Well, no," said Frog. He hadn't *seen* it but he had heard it. They talked about ghosts and monsters and other ghastly things for a long time.

Pig made some breakfast.
"You know," said Hare. "Everyone is frightened sometimes."
"Even you?" asked Frog surprised.

"Oh yes," said Hare. "I was very frightened this morning when I thought you were lost."
There was a silence.

Then everyone laughed.
"Don't be ridiculous, Hare," said Frog. "You have nothing
to fear. We are always here."

Andersen Press paperback picture books

FRANKIE MAKES A FRIEND
by Tony Bradman & Sonia Holleyman

SCRUMPY
by Elizabeth Dale & Frédéric Joos

I HATE MY TEDDY BEAR
David McKee

EMERGENCY MOUSE
by Bernard Stone & Ralph Steadman

FROG IN WINTER
by Max Velthuijs

FROG AND THE STRANGER
by Max Velthuijs

FROG IS FRIGHTENED
by Max Velthuijs

THE GREAT GREEN MOUSE DISASTER
by Martin Waddell & Philippe Dupasquier

THE TALE OF GEORGIE GRUB
by Jeanne Willis & Margaret Chamberlain

THE TALE OF MUCKY MABEL
by Jeanne Willis & Margaret Chamberlain